"Can Teddy have a new bed too?" asked Milly.

Mum unpacked the big boxes.

First experier

Big Bed

W
FRANKLIN WATTS
NEW YORK • LONDON • SYDNEY

"Wake up, Milly," said Mum. "Your new bed is here."

"I've got just the right box for Teddy's bed," said Milly.

"I can't find the hammer. Can you see it anywhere?" frowned Mum.

Mum twisted the screws into the wood. "Oh, dear!" she said, "this is hard work."

Milly was very busy gluing Teddy's new bed.

"Phew, your new bed is ready now," said Mum at last.

"So is Teddy's," Milly smiled proudly.

Milly had great fun bouncing on her big bed.

"Isn't it BIG!" said Milly.
"I can't wait for it to be night."

"Mum, Teddy wants to know if he can have a story in his new bed?"

"Of course he can," smiled Mum.
"Would you like to help him
to choose one?"

Milly and Teddy snuggled down
in their new beds.

Goodnight, Milly.
Goodnight, Teddy.

Make a bed for your Teddy.

Find a shoe box and
a long piece of card.

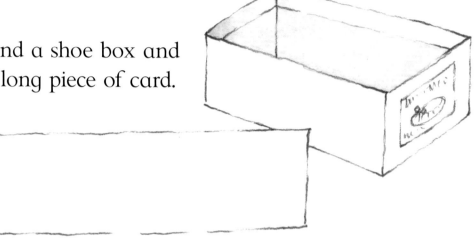

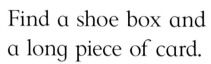

Decorate the box and the card
with paint or sticky shapes.

Fold the card in half and
then open it out again.

Glue the edges of the card to
one end of your box.
Then leave it to dry.

Now you can snuggle your
Teddy into his new bed.
Find some bits of material
for blankets.

Sharing books with your child

Early Worms are a range of books for you to share with your child. Together you can look at the pictures and talk about the subject or story. Listening, looking and talking are the first vital stages in children's reading development, and lay the early foundation for good reading habits.

Talking about the pictures is the first step in involving children in the pages of a book, especially if the subject or story can be related to their own familiar world. When children can relate the matter in the book to their own experience, this can be used as a starting point for introducing new knowledge, whether it is counting, getting to know colours or finding out how other people live.

Gradually children will develop their listening and concentration skills as well as a sense of what a book is. Soon they will learn how a book works: that you turn the pages from right to left, and read the story from left to right on a double page. They start to realize that the black marks on the page have a meaning and that they relate to the pictures. Once children have grasped these basic essentials they will develop strategies for "decoding" the text such as matching words and pictures, and recognising the rhythm of the language in order to predict what comes next. Soon they will start to take over the role of an independent reader, handling and looking at books even if they can't yet read the words.

Most important of all, children should realize that books are a source of pleasure. This stems from your reading sessions which are times of mutual enjoyment and shared experience. It is then that children find the key to becoming real readers.